For daydreamers,
big and small

With special thanks
to my kids

Written and illustrated by

# Elly MacKay

# In the
# Clouds

tundra

*H*ello, little friend!

Are you as bored as I am?

Don't clouds ruin everything?

Is the sun shining
above the clouds?

Will you take me there?

How high can birds fly?

Why are clouds so far away?

How do they float?

And where do they go when they disappear?

Why does something so huge feel like nothing at all?

And how do clouds
carry the rain?

Do you think islands float on water

like clouds float in the sky?

Or are they all connected down below?

Are we connected too?

Do you think clouds have memories?

Can they remember the dinosaurs?

Allosaurus?

Stegosaurus?

Diplodocus?

The names of clouds sound a bit like dinosaur names . . .

Cirrus . . .

Cumulus . . .

Stratus . . .

I can never remember them all . . .

Or tell the clouds apart.

But if clouds were shaped like dinosaurs,

I could name them by heart!

Do you think there are clouds on other planets?

If so, are they as beautiful as ours?

If clouds have traveled around the whole world,
and all through time, do you think they've
ever seen another bird like you?
Or a girl like me?

Do you wonder about things too?

Like, when the sea meets the sky,

how do you know where to fly?

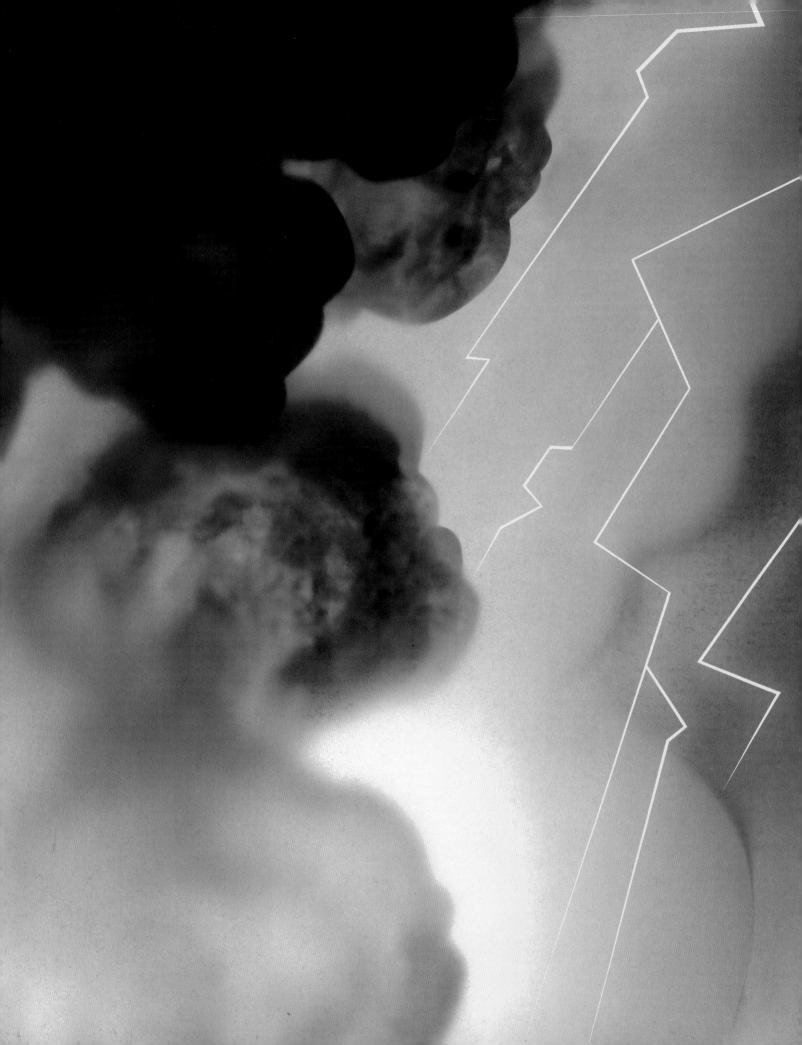

And if you get lost in a cloud,
how do you know where to go?

*Boom!*

Whoooooaa . . .

How did you learn to fly like that?

You're as quick as lightning!

You're the Queen of the Sky!

You're almost home!

We made it!

Is your heart beating as fast as mine?

Aren't clouds WONDROUS?

I have so many questions, don't you?

*Chirp-chirp*

You do? What is it?!

*Cheer-cheer-cheerio-cheer-cheer?*

My orange? Oh, sure, help yourself.

Can you tell how close a storm is from looking at the clouds? Once you see a storm cloud, also called a nimbus cloud, keep your eyes and ears open. Lightning comes first, followed by thunder. If you see lightning then hear thunder within 30 seconds, it is closer than 10 km, or 6 mi, away. Seek shelter!

**Can birds fly above the clouds?** Yes, many larger birds such as ducks and geese do. Even some small songbirds fly above the clouds when they migrate.

**Why are clouds so far away? How do they float?** Clouds are made of tiny water droplets. The droplets are so spread out that gravity has little effect and warm air from below lifts them upward.

**Where do clouds go when they disappear?** When the liquid water droplets that form clouds evaporate, they turn into gas, which is no longer visible.

**How much do clouds weigh? What would it feel like to touch a cloud?** An average cumulus cloud weighs the same as 100 elephants. You've likely walked through a cloud — fog is a cloud that hugs the ground! The tiny water droplets are so small that they don't feel like anything at all.

**How do clouds carry the rain?** Clouds can hold a great deal of water. They are held up by the wind, but when the water droplets get large enough, gravity pulls them down to earth.

**Are clouds alive?** No. But there are types of bacteria that live in the clouds!

**When is the best day to spot a cloud shaped like a dinosaur, a fish or even a girl?** The best days to search for shapes in the clouds are sunny days with puffy cumulus clouds.

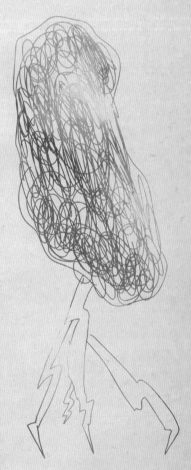

**Are there clouds on other planets?** There are clouds on other planets, but they aren't like our clouds. Saturn has clouds of sulfuric acid! And on Jupiter, there is liquid helium rain! Some scientists think that the clouds of Saturn may rain diamonds.

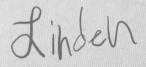

# Sources

How Stuff Works: Does it rain on other planets?
https://science.howstuffworks.com/rain-other-planets.htm

INO Technologies: The Correct Way to Estimate Lightning Strike Distance
https://inotechnologies.com/correct-estimate-lightning-distance/

LiveScience: Earth's Clouds Alive with Bacteria
https://www.livescience.com/2333-earth-clouds-alive-bacteria.html

LiveScience: How High Can Birds Fly?
https://www.livescience.com/55455-how-high-can-birds-fly.html

*Mental Floss*: How Much Does a Cloud Weigh?
https://www.mentalfloss.com/article/49786/how-much-does-cloud-weigh

NASA: Why Don't Clouds Fall Out of the Sky?
https://pumas.nasa.gov/examples/why-dont-clouds-fall-out-sky

UCSB ScienceLine: Are there clouds on other planets?
http://scienceline.ucsb.edu/getkey.php?key=884

Library and Archives Canada Cataloguing in Publication

Title: In the clouds / Elly MacKay.
Names: MacKay, Elly, author.
Identifiers: Canadiana (print) 20210090766 | Canadiana (ebook) 20210090790 |
ISBN 9780735266964 (hardcover) | ISBN 9780735266971 (EPUB)
Classification: LCC PS8625.K38845 I5 2022 | DDC jC813/.6—dc23

Published simultaneously in the United States of America by Tundra Books of Northern New York, an imprint of Penguin Random House Canada Young Readers, a division of Penguin Random House of Canada Limited

Library of Congress Control Number: 2020951762

Edited by Tara Walker with assistance from Margot Blankier
Designed by Kelly Hill
The illustrations in this book are photographs of paper dioramas.
The portrait on the first spread is a photograph of Hans Christian Andersen.
The drawings in the back matter were created by Koen MacKay.
The text was set in Requiem.

Printed in China

www.penguinrandomhouse.ca

1  2  3  4  5    26  25  24  23  22